Richard Musman

ESCAPE IN NEW YORK

Ernst Klett Schulbuchverlag
Stuttgart Düsseldorf Berlin Leipzig

Acknowledgements: Bavaria, München, (Frank) p. 49, (Rostek) p. 35, (Schmied) p. 32; Bilderdienst Süddeutscher Verlag, München p. 16, p. 20, (Kummels) cover, p. 12, p. 24 (Lehnartz) p. 27; DPA, Düsseldorf p. 39; Musman, Steep p. 4, p.11, p. 17, p. 23, p. 30, p. 34, p. 44; Shostal Associates, New York p. 25; Ullstein, Berlin, (Lehnartz) p. 9, (Wernicke) p. 37

Gedruckt auf Papier aus
chlorfrei gebleichtem Zellstoff,
säurefrei.

1. Auflage 1 16 15 14 | 1998 97

Alle Drucke dieser Auflage können im Unterricht nebeneinander benutzt werden, sie sind untereinander unverändert. Die letzte Zahl bezeichnet das Jahr des Druckes.

Kartographie: G. Wustmann, Mötzingen.
Umschlaggestaltung: Gebhardt und Lorenz, Korntal.
Druck: Gutmann + Co., Talheim. Printed in Germany.
ISBN 3-12-542600-6

Contents

The coffee shop

1. A Meeting at Niagara Falls

The coffee shop was empty. Kevin pushed the cup away from him and placed his arms on the counter. He had just left school and was off to New York in a week's time to be a tourist guide. He had spent a year in New York when he was fifteen and knew the city well. His Aunt Bella, with whom he was going to stay, had found him the job, and he had had no difficulty in getting a work permit.

A boy and a girl came into the coffee shop. "Hi, Kev!" "Hi, Di! Hi, Doug!" Everyone liked Kevin, but his friends knew that there were moments when he wanted to be left alone. Doug and Di passed him by and sat down at a table near the window. Kevin was thinking of his mother. She was going to marry a Toronto businessman whom he did not like. He had told his mother exactly what he thought of his future stepfather. She had replied that it was none of his business. "O.K.,

Mom! Marry him, but don't expect me to come and live with you." "Do what you like, Kev," she had said. He did not want to live alone in the house in Niagara Falls, so he had written to his Aunt Bella. He and Aunt Bella were great friends.

The thunder of the waterfall reminded him that the only thing that was interesting in Niagara Falls, Canada, was the Falls! There was nothing to keep him at home. It was at that moment that he saw opposite him, on the other side of the counter, a girl he had never seen before. She had a heart-shaped face and a large mouth. Her hair was very dark and fell below her ears. A black fringe hung halfway down her forehead.

"Want anything else, Kev?" asked Betty, the girl behind the counter. He and Betty had been at school together. She was pretty, but she had nothing interesting to talk about. He shook his head and looked again at the girl across the counter. Her eyes, which were a bright blue, were full of anxiety, and she kept looking towards the door as if she was expecting an unwelcome visitor.

"Hi!" he said, walking round the counter and sitting down beside her.

The girl looked at him with surprise. "Hi!" she said.

"Let me get you a coffee," he said, "or do you want something to eat?"

She smiled. "I don't know why you are doing this. You don't know me."

"Well, I'll be honest with you. You look as though you're in trouble. I wondered if perhaps I could help you."

She looked straight into his eyes. "You know, I could be rather angry. A complete stranger interfering in somebody else's affairs! It isn't usual, is it?"

"No, it isn't. But when I see somebody I think looks especially nice, I try to make friends – to see if I was right! No, but I *do* think you're in trouble, and I *would* like to help you if you'll let me."

She smiled. "Well you're honest! But you can't help me, I'm afraid, and I'd rather not talk about it, if you don't mind. I'll have that cup of coffee, though. Let's go and sit at a table. It's more comfortable."

Betty smiled to herself as she came to take their order. She would have liked to be in the girl's place, instead of serving her. But Kev had never been interested in her.

"Just two cups of coffee, please, Betty," Kevin said.

"O.K., *sir*!" Betty said.

"Where do you come from?" Kevin asked the girl.

"New York."

"Is that where you've come from now?"

"No. I'm still at school. I go to a boarding school twenty miles from Niagara. It's called Saint Cecilia's. Have you heard of it?"

"No. Is it one of those schools for rich girls?"

"Yes, but I hate it! If I wasn't able to read a lot of books, I don't know what I'd do."

"Have you run away from school, then?"

"No – it's the first day of the vacation."

She looked straight into his eyes. He leaned across the table.

"I'm Kevin Patterson. I live here in Niagara Falls. What's your name?"

"Cathy."

"Cathy who?"

"Cathy O'Brien."

They shook hands.

"Why won't you tell me what's the matter, Cathy?"

She did not answer for a moment, and then she spoke in such a low voice that he could hardly hear her. "Because if you knew, it might get you into serious trouble."

"I'll risk it. Please tell me! I don't like mysteries between friends."

"No. Please don't talk about it again." She looked out the window. "Don't you get tired of that awful noise – the Falls, I mean?"

"No, I guess we're used to it."

Betty brought two cups and poured in the coffee. Then, when Kevin did not look at her, she gave him a kick under the table. Kevin did not notice.

"How is it your eyes are blue when your hair is so dark, Cathy?"

"That often happens with Irish people. My mother was Irish. My father was an Irish American."

"Are your parents dead?"

"Yes. My mother died when my brother was born. I was ten then. My father married again, but he died when I was twelve."

"So you were brought up by your stepmother?"

She hesitated. "Well, I live with her. My brother is luckier. He's been brought up by my grandmother in Charleston, South Carolina. I hardly ever see him, and that makes me very sad."

"How old are you, Cathy?"

"Seventeen."

"Me too. I'll be eighteen next month. I've just left High School. I'm going to be a guide for Swift's Tours in New York for a year. Do you know them?"

She shook her head.

"I know New York well. I spent a year there when I was fifteen. We must meet. I'll be there next week. Tell me your address."

She looked down at the table. "No, I don't think that would be safe. But I'd love to see you. Why don't you give me *your* address?"

"Sure!" Kevin answered.

Suddenly he saw her freeze. The coffee-shop door had opened, and a middle-aged woman was coming towards them. Her face was heavy, and her straight brown hair had been cut short above her ears. She wore knee-high black boots and a thick grey coat. She looked rather like a soldier.

"Your stepmother?" Kevin said in a low voice.

"Yes."

The stepmother stood beside Cathy, who sat quite still, not looking at her.

"I told you to meet me at the car at 4.30. It's now 5 o'clock. What have you been doing?"

She looked suspiciously at Kevin. "Who's this?" she asked Cathy.

"A Canadian friend," Cathy answered.

"You make friends quickly, I see! What's his name?"

"Rob Masterman," Cathy lied, without a moment's hesitation.

Kevin got up and held out his hand, but the stepmother let it hang in the air. She looked at him for a long time, as if she wanted to remember his face. Then she took Cathy's arm and pulled her to her feet.

"Come on, child! We're late."

Holding Cathy's arm firmly in hers, she marched to the door. Cathy turned back and looked hard at Kevin. He was sure that she was asking him for help. He nodded his head, trying to make her understand that he would look for her in New York. She disappeared, and a moment later Kevin heard the roar of a powerful car. The stepmother was clearly in a hurry. But where was she going?

"What was all that about?" Betty asked. "Who was that awful woman?"

"Her stepmother."

"Poor kid!"

"You're darned right!"

"Look!" Betty said suddenly. "She has left her bag behind."

Kevin picked it up. It was quite an ordinary bag, black and rather old.

"Let's see what's inside," Betty said.

Kevin opened it and found only a handkerchief and a purse with a few coins in it, and a key. That was all.

"It must be the key to her front door in New York – in Manhattan, the Bronx, Brooklyn, Queens? Where could it be?"

"Why do you want to find her?"

"Because she's rather special, I think, and she's in some sort of trouble. I'd like to help her."

"She probably just hates her stepmother. You can't do anything about that."

"No! I'm sure she's in serious trouble."

"You've been watching too much TV! Cops and robbers!"

"Maybe you're right, Betty. Give me my check, please."

He paid and went back to his empty home. His mother was in Toronto. She was not coming back. It would be almost a week before he was in New York. That was too long to wait. He sat down at the phone and called Aunt Bella.

"O.K. if I come on Thursday instead of Sunday, Auntie?"

"Of course, darling!" Aunt Bella said. "Come any time you like. It can't be very nice living alone in that house."

2. Journey to New York

The next day, Kevin packed his rucksack and put Cathy's key in an inside pocket of his jacket. Then he went to the bank. He changed into American dollars all the money he had, and then walked to the bridge which crossed the border.

It was a warm spring afternoon when he crossed the bridge to the American side of the Falls. Far below he could see the little ship, *Maid*

The George Washington Bridge

of the Mist, crowded with tourists, moving slowly towards the world's greatest waterfall. He had once wanted to be captain of the *Maid of the Mist . . .*

The Immigration Officer on the American side of the bridge knew him and let him through at once. He went into a truck-stop and asked if anyone would give him a lift to New York.

"O.K., kid, I'll take you," said a cheerful young Texan on his way to New Jersey.

They drove through the night, stopping twice at all-night truck-stops. Adam was in a hurry and, unlike most of the cars they passed, drove much faster than the 55 mph speed limit. They reached the suburbs of New York City at 6 o'clock in the morning.

"What part of New York do you want, kid?"

"Greenwich Village."

"O.K. I'll take you as far as the George Washington Bridge."

He stopped near the bridge.

"This is it, kid."

"Thanks, Adam."

"Be seein' you, Kev."

Kevin walked across the great bridge. The sun was coming up, but was not yet shining on the broad Hudson River. As he walked slowly through Fort Washington Park, a policeman came up behind him.

"What's a kid like you doin' here at this hour?"

"Just walking. I'm allowed to, aren't I?"

"Sure, it's allowed! Where you from?"

"Niagara Falls, Canada."

"Let's see your passport."

The policeman looked at it carefully and then gave it back to him.

"How did you get here?"

"On a truck."

"Hitch-hiking on freeways is not allowed. You know that?"

"No, I didn't."

More and more commuters were beginning to cross the George Washington Bridge and drive on down the Parkway to the center of Manhattan. Americans start work early.

"If you're hoping to get work, you know what'll happen to you if you don't have a permit?"

"I do have a permit."

He showed it to the policeman.

The policeman looked at Kevin's clothes and his well-cut blond hair. "Why didn't you come by air, or by Greyhound? You don't look poor."

"I didn't have enough money."

"Where you goin' now, then?"

"To my aunt's house in Greenwich Village."

"O. K., but don't do anything stupid while you're in New York," he said, and walked away through the park.

It was now nearly 7 o'clock. Kevin walked to the nearest subway station on 168/Broadway. He gave the clerk 3 dollars and received six

Subway tokens

tokens. He dropped one in the turnstile slot and went down to the trains. It was easy to get lost in the subway until you understood it, but it was the cheapest way of traveling. For fifty cents you could travel from one end of New York to the other. An express roared through the station on the center track and a few minutes later the local train came in. It was the rush hour, so he had to push his way into the crowded car. He changed at Columbus Circle and finally came up into Manhattan just off Fifth Avenue. He had decided not to go straight to Aunt Bella's. He wanted to feel what New York was like again. He had spent a very happy year there.

As he wandered among the people on Fifth Avenue, Kevin began to think of Cathy. He looked for her among the hurrying crowd. Strange things did sometimes happen! Two well-dressed blacks crossed in front of him. And then he saw her. She was only a few yards in front of him. He

Subway exit on 5th Avenue

Sidewalk scene in Washington Square

knew it was her, the way she walked, the dark hair which fell below her ears. He called out, "Cathy!" and began to run. As he came up beside her, a pretty woman of about forty turned and smiled at him when she saw his disappointment.

"Excuse me!" he said.

He left Fifth Avenue and looked for a cheap coffee shop where he could have breakfast. Aunt Bella's breakfasts were not large enough for him. He sat at the counter and ordered two fried eggs, over hard, with hash browns and a cup of coffee, which the waitress filled up three times at no extra cost.

"You're Canadian, aren't you?" she asked. "I can tell from the accent."

"Yeah!" he replied. "Niagara Falls."

It was 9 o'clock, time to go and say "Hi!" to Aunt Bella. He went down into the subway again and got out at Washington Square. The streets of Greenwich Village were quiet and empty compared with the crowds and noise of the great Avenues. Children were playing beneath the trees of the Square, while students hurried across it to their lectures in New York University. He stood for a moment under the great Washington Arch and looked up Fifth Avenue. It was very broad and straight, and was so long that he could not see to the end of it. It ran right down the center of Manhattan. Then he walked down the little tree-lined street where Aunt Bella had her apartment. The house had only three floors, and Aunt Bella owned the top two. He climbed the steps to the street door on the second floor and rang the bell.

When Aunt Bella saw him standing there, she threw her arms around him.

"Kevin! It's lovely to see you. Have you had breakfast? Of course you have! I'd forgotten. You don't like my breakfasts, do you? I'll have to get some more eggs. How's your mother?"

"She's going to marry that guy!"

Aunt Bella and her sister-in-law were not great friends.

"Well, if it makes her happy . . ."

Aunt Bella was between forty and fifty. She liked to change the color of her hair. At the moment it was red, and her chocolate-colored shirt hung over bright purple pants. People loved her. She spent her whole life and much of her money – she was not rich – in trying to help the many different peoples of the great city.

"Just come and go as you like," she said. "You won't see much of me. You know that."

Kevin smiled. He understood his aunt and loved her.

"Which group are you working for now, Auntie?"

"The Puerto Ricans. Their life is very difficult. Many of them can't get jobs because they don't speak English well enough. You know, some Americans are unpleasant to people who don't speak English well. Here's a spare door key. The bed's ready in the little room upstairs. Now I have to write a letter."

She sat down at her desk. Kevin admired his aunt and her enthusiasm. There were so many different peoples and races in New York. There were whole streets where Italians lived together. In fact, more Italians lived in New York than in Rome, more Jews than in Tel-Aviv. There were more than a million blacks and Puerto Ricans. Then there were the Irish Americans, who still called themselves Irish and still hated the English. He hoped Cathy wasn't a racist. He felt sure she wasn't. He sat on the couch for a while, dreaming. Then he fetched the telephone book which had names beginning with 'O'. He soon shut the book. It was hopeless. There were hundreds of O'Briens. He shut the book with such a bang that Aunt Bella looked up from her desk.

"What's the matter, Kev? Who are you looking for in that telephone book? A girlfriend?"

"Well, sort of."

He told his aunt everything that had happened and she listened very carefully. He was sure she would have some very useful ideas. She

OBRIEN **MANHATTAN**

O'Brien George 166 E63 753-1056
O'Brien Geo B 2 TudrCtyPl 986-5114
O'Brien Gerald F 7 PeterCooperRd 228-5229
O'Brien Gerard J lwyr 61 Bway 269-6845
O'Brien Gerard T 615 E14 674-7148
O'Brien Glenn 14 W88 724-6902
O'Brien Gordon 1623 3Av 427-3768
Obrien H 20 ParkAv 889-3730
O'Brien H 1484 2Av 737-4377
O'Brien H E 420 E23 228-7348
O'Brien H S 8 E83 737-0886
O'Brien Helen 1737 YorkAv 369-0979
O'Brien Helen A 435 W23 243-1708
O'Brien Helen M 136 W75 874-5237
O'Brien Henry J 529 W111 864-8141
O'Brien Herbert 31 E12 477-5069
O'Brien Hod 308 W104 749-4005
O'Brien Hugh P 407 E69 535-7801
O'Brien I 548 RivDr 662-8490
O'Brien I 1780 1Av 860-2983
O'Brien I J 653 E14 674-4698
O'Brien I V 444 2Av 683-8973
O'Brien International Assocs
450 ParkAv 826-2949
O'Brien J 195 ClarmntAv 749-2792
O'Brien J 97 LexAv 679-3052
O'Brien J 986-3832
O'Brien J 100 Thayer 569-8281
O'Brien J 330 E65 249-0702
O'Brien J 307 W89 595-4641
O'Brien J F 753-1573
O'Brien J J 1670 YorkAv 988-7079
O'Brien J Joseph chirprctr
28 Revere Dr W FlrlPk 516 354-6016

O'Brien J M 310 1Av 228-4262
O'Brien J M 570 W190 928-8202
O'Brien J P 1233 YorkAv 861-5008
O'Brien J T&Assoc Inc 211 E43 697-2306
O'Brien Jack G 131 RivDr 873-7542
O'Brien Jack T 225 E46 753-7407
O'Brien Jas 1492 LexAv 876-8848
O'Brien James 328 E 9 673-5058
O'Brien James 250 E87 722-2343
O'Brien Jas 166 E90 289-5715
O'Brien James A 1010 5Av 861-8274
O'Brien James F 444 E20 228-8742
O'Brien James F 436 W27 695-6324
O'Brien James F lwyr 61 Bway 480-0400
O'Brien Jas G cabnt mkr
149 Avenue A 228-4210
O'Brien Jas J 256 SeamanAv 942-9436
O'Brien Jas J 515 W111 864-0485
O'BRIEN JAMES J PE 1 CherryHill
CherryHillNJ **NYC Tel No 689-8260**
O'BRIEN JAMES J PE 8 W40 **689-8260**
O'Brien James J pe 8 W40 921-9898
O'Brien James M 150 E93 427-8673
O'Brien James R 328 W19 691-7715
O'Brien Jas V consultant 233 Bway 962-2811
O'Brien James W 165 W91 595-5149
O'Brien Jeanne M 435 W23 243-1708
O'Brien Jere F 235 E22 686-8680
O'Brien Jeremiah 525 E82 737-8207
O'Brien Jeremiah Jr 153 W74 877-2588
O'Brien Joan S atty
1185 AvenueAmericas 869-8460
O'Brien John 1 AdrianAv 562-8765
O'Brien John 68 CabriniBlvd 781-5209

thought for a moment. Then she suddenly said, "You were talking about a boarding school she went to in upstate New York. Did she tell you its name?"

"Yes. It was Saint something . . . something beginning with S or C."

"Get me the Buffalo book," Aunt Bella said. "Thank you. Now then . . . Well, I can only see one boarding school beginning with 'Saint'. Was it Saint Cecilia's?"

"Yes, it was. Auntie, you're wonderful!"

"No, darling. I use my imagination. That's all!"

"Do you think they would really give us her home address?"

"They might not if you called. But if I called and said I was an old friend of the family, I think they would."

"It's the vacation. Do you think anyone will still be there?"

"I think the secretary will still be there. Anyway, I'll try, honey."

"Thank you, Auntie!"

Aunt Bella's voice, as she talked to the secretary, was all honey. "Oh, thank you so much, it's real kind of you. Not at all! Goodbye!"

She wrote the address down on a card and gave it to Kevin.

"You sure know how to act, Auntie. I didn't know you were as good as that."

"I'm good at everything, honey!"

"You sure are!"

She became suddenly serious. "You say the girl is in trouble, Kev. You realize the neighborhood in which she lives is not exactly smart? That part of the West Side can even be dangerous, especially at night. It's a poor neighborhood. A cop was murdered there the other night."

"I'll be careful, Auntie."

"I know you, Kev. You don't know what the word means!"

"I'm nearly three years older now."

"Maybe, maybe! But I must finish my letter. I've found some books on New York which may be a help to you. They're on the table by the couch."

3. The Search for Cathy begins

Aunt Bella blew him a kiss and left. He lay on the couch, turning over the pages of a not very interesting book on New York. "New York is held together by 65 bridges. The Brooklyn Bridge is the oldest suspension bridge in the world . . .". He imagined he was on Brooklyn Bridge with a party of tourists . . . "And did you know, folks, that the engineer who built the Brooklyn Bridge died after an accident while the bridge was being built? And later his son became paralyzed? He stayed too long under the water while he was examining the bottom of the bridge. But the bridge sure does look pretty at night when all its lights are on . . . "

Brooklyn Bridge

He turned over a few more pages . . . "You know, folks, there's no place called the 'Big Apple'. New York is the Big Apple – Rockefeller Center, Broadway, all the great Avenues, the Harlem ghetto with its awful slums, the United Nations building, Chinatown, the Hudson River – the whole exciting, beautiful place called New York. That's the Big Apple." He shut the book with a bang. He was not afraid of being a guide. He liked people, and they liked him.

He got up and walked up and down the room. Then, making a quick decision, he called Cathy's number.

"Yes? Who is it?"

He recognized Mrs. O'Brien's voice at once.

"We met at Niagara Falls, do you remember?"

"You're Rob Masterman?"

"Er . . . yes, that's right. I promised Cathy I'd call her when I got to New York."

Mrs. O'Brien tried to stop him, but Kevin talked straight on.

"I wonder if I could talk to Cathy? You see, I'm starting work in three days' time. She . . ."

"I'm sorry," Mrs. O'Brien said in a hard voice, "Cathy doesn't want to see you. So please don't call again."

She put down the telephone receiver without waiting for him to answer. He was more than ever sure that Cathy's trouble was something to do with her stepmother. He looked at his watch. It was 11.30. He decided to go to the apartment house and ask at the desk to see Cathy. He was sure that the stepmother would not allow him to see her, but he might learn something interesting.

He went out into the cool spring air. It was a beautiful day. The windows of the skyscrapers which rose high above the old red houses of Washington Square shone like jewels in the sunshine. He reached the subway station and went down to the trains. When the train came in there was only standing room, and he stood among a group of blacks and Puerto Ricans. New Yorkers who were rich never took the subway.

At last he reached his station. He came out on Eighth Avenue. It was one of the poorer districts of Manhattan. He passed small stores and offices, bars and cheap restaurants. When he reached the street which he guessed led down to the O'Brien's apartment house on Eleventh Avenue, he turned left. He could see at the bottom of the street a big new building. It was not like other buildings in Manhattan. It was taller than all the buildings around it, but it was not a skyscraper. It was about

Poor area on Manhattan Island

thirty stories high and very wide. The houses along the street had been built in the mid-nineteenth century, so New Yorkers called them old. People with money had once lived in them, but now there were only poor whites and poor blacks. At the end of the street, opposite the high wall of the apartment house, the houses were empty and many of the doors and windows were broken. Eleventh Avenue was even less smart than Eighth Avenue. The buildings were three or four stories high, and all kinds of advertisements had been stuck on the walls.

The main entrance to the apartment house was on Eleventh Avenue. It was very different from what he had expected. He could see at once that the apartments belonged to people with money. Cathy must have a fine view of the Hudson River and the docks where the cruise liners lay, for the number of her apartment was 908, and that meant that it was on the ninth floor. He walked down Eleventh Avenue, trying to decide what to do. He reached the Lincoln Tunnel, one of the two great tunnels connecting New York with New Jersey. Trucks, yellow cabs, Lincolns, Chevelles, traffic of all kinds, disappeared under the Hudson River. At last he decided to do what he had at first intended to do – ask to see Cathy.

Kevin went back to the apartment house and walked straight through the glass doors into the lobby. He was surprised at what he saw. Between the lobby and the elevators there were two locked turnstiles which could only be opened by the people who lived there, or by the security guard. On the desk lay an open book and a telephone, and behind the desk stood a security guard who looked as if he had once been a policeman. Kevin had never seen anything quite like this. He knew that in the smart apartment houses people had special locks on their doors, and little holes through which they could look at their visitors. He knew, too, that there were sometimes muggings in the elevators and even in offices. But he had never heard of locked turnstiles before.

He went up to the security guard who, he was glad to find, gave him a friendly smile.

"What can I do for you, kid?"

"I'd like to see Cathy O'Brien, please."

"Oh, you would, would you? And who shall I say you are?"

Kevin was just going to say 'Rob Masterman', when he remembered his identity card.

"Kevin Patterson," he said.

The guard held out his hand. "Come on, Kevin Patterson! Let's see your identity card."

Kevin showed it to him.

"O.K.! I'll call the apartment."

The guard picked up the phone. "That Mrs. O'Brien? There's a young man here who says his name is Kevin Patterson. He'd like to see Cathy . . . She's gone to find out if she'll see you," he told Kevin. "Mrs. O'Brien? She will see him? . . . She'll be down in a minute? Oh, sure! He'll wait!"

Kevin was very surprised, but said nothing. A few minutes later, he heard the elevator doors opening – and saw Mrs. O'Brien coming towards him on the other side of the turnstiles.

"Kevin Patterson! Rob Masterman! Did you really think you'd trick me with a false name?" She turned to the security guard. "Which is his real name?"

"His identity card says Kevin Patterson."

"Can't you get it into your thick head that you aren't going to see my stepdaughter? Now just go away, and don't ever come back."

"Why? I think Cathy would like to see me."

"Don't talk to me like that!" she said angrily. Then she turned to the security guard. "Get rid of him, please!"

The guard, who was now no longer friendly, came from behind the desk, took Kevin by the arm and threw him out the door into the street.

"Next time you come round here, I'll call the police."

As Kevin got up, he saw through the glass doors a black man standing in the middle of the lobby and staring at him. The man turned his back immediately he saw Kevin looking at him. But Kevin knew that he would recognize him again at once, because he was completely bald.

He walked back up the street. The neighborhood was unpleasant, and he wanted to get out of it as quickly as possible. There was no one in the lower part of the street, except a few children playing among the empty, damaged houses. At the top end, women were talking together on their doorsteps. They did not turn and look at him as he passed. He crossed avenue after avenue until he reached Sixth Avenue. Rockefeller Center was quite near. He sat down under one of the gold-colored umbrellas and ordered a hot chocolate. There were people of all kinds at the tables around him. There were young men in jeans, like him. There were girls, too, who were wearing jeans. There were smartly dressed ladies who had come to Manhattan to shop, and a few busi-

nessmen who had left their skyscraper offices for a late coffee-break.

Afterwards he walked past Radio City Music Hall, which he had visited many times during his earlier stay in New York. It was built in the thirties, but was still the largest movie house in the world. It was showing the latest horror movie. He remembered the great Wurlitzer organ, the largest of its kind in the world, and in the interval there were the Rockettes dancing girls, who danced with the discipline of well-trained soldiers. He stopped at a snack bar for a hot dog, and then walked up Broadway to Times Square, one of the most famous centers of New York, but one of the least pleasant. There were advertisements on all the buildings. There were also many small movie houses with large, colored posters, which, it was hoped, would tempt people to enter. Further along Broadway, between Times Square and Lincoln Center, he passed the Swift's Tours office, where he would soon be working. He looked in the window and noticed the tours they were advertising, but he did not go in. By now his feet were sore, but he walked on to Lincoln Center, where he hoped to get tickets for a concert or an opera but they were all too expensive.

Kevin arrived back at Aunt Bella's at 4.30 and threw himself on the couch. Aunt Bella listened without a smile when he told her what had happened at the apartment house, and about the bald-headed black in the lobby.

"Well, if you're sensible, which you're not, you'll have nothing more to do with Cathy O'Brien. Take her stepmother's warning seriously. I don't want to learn one day that my beloved nephew has been murdered."

Kevin sat up. "Are you being serious, Auntie?"

"Completely! I know people talk too much about the dangers of New York. But there *are* gangs, and there *are* muggers, and sometimes ordinary people get hurt. It wouldn't surprise me if your Cathy's stepmother hasn't something to do with a gang."

"Perhaps you're right, Auntie, but I don't think Cathy is part of it."

"Maybe not, but that doesn't make it any safer for you."

Kevin looked his aunt in the eyes. "Auntie, you know I'm always honest with you. I'm going to go on finding out what I can. If I find out anything really dangerous, then I'll go to the police. I promise you! Try not to worry."

"O.K." Aunt Bella said. "I can't stop you, and I won't try, but you can't stop me worrying. All I can say is, 'good luck', and please ask me if you want any help."

They stared at each other without smiling, which did not happen very often. Then Kevin went up to his aunt and kissed her.

"I'll try and be careful, Auntie. I promise you."

This time Aunt Bella did smile. "You're quite your father's son. He was just as crazy as you!"

4. Kevin tries again

The next morning Kevin said to his aunt, "I'm going to the apartment house again. If something happens, I thought you would want to know . . . I'm sure it won't, but . . . "

Aunt Bella got up without a word, opened the telephone book and wrote down a number in her note book. "That's the nearest police precinct," she said. Her face was unsmiling.

"That's a good idea, Auntie," Kevin replied.

Aunt Bella laughed. "Maybe you're not so like your father after all. He would have told me it was nothing to do with me!"

Kevin reached the apartment house at 10.30. This time he stood close to the wall of one of the empty buildings across the road. Black women and white women, some of them holding small children by the hand, came out the building with their shopping baskets. A big New York garbage truck stopped in front of him and lifted the garbage from the sidewalk. But nothing else passed either up or down the street. Black children were running in and out the empty houses, playing games.

Time passed. He looked at his watch. It was already 12.30, and he was getting hungry. Did Mrs. O'Brien know that he was there? He looked up at the shining wall of windows. Was her apartment on this side or the other side of the building?

Kevin waited another half-hour and then decided to give up. He was walking back up the street, when he heard the sound of a car behind him. He turned, but it was difficult to see the person behind the driving wheel, because the sun was shining on the windshield. The car, a dirty ten-year-old Oldsmobile, was driving on the wrong side of the road, beside the sidewalk on which he was walking. It was less than twenty yards behind him. As he looked back, the car turned quickly towards him, driving at great speed. Kevin just had time to throw himself through the door of one of the empty houses. The car hit the wall of the house, but was thrown back onto the road again. It disappeared up the street.

Kevin had cut his face and hands when he fell. There was dust all over his clothes. There was dust in his eyes, too. He sat up rubbing them. When his eyes were clear, he saw a young black woman looking down at him.

"That man sure tried to kill you. He's crazy!"

"Can you tell me what he was like?"

"Sure! He's black, but he's got some white in him, too, and he sure is bald!"

"Do you know him, then?"

"Do I know him! Everyone knows him – everyone that's black, I mean."

"Would you give evidence against him, if the police caught him?"

"Oh, no, man! I couldn't do that. It would be kind of signing my death warrant. In this city most killings are black folks killing black folks. I'd say I never saw nothing. I sure am sorry, honey, but that's the way it is. Come with me. I'll clean you up."

Kevin followed her into her first floor apartment. She had two young children, and only two rooms. There was hardly any furniture, except one king-size bed. To get hot water, she had to boil a kettle on the stove. There was no bathroom and no bathtub. When the water was hot enough, she cleaned his cuts and washed the dirt from his face.

"Maybe you ought to see a doctor," she said. "Those cuts are real bad."

"No, I'll be O.K., thank you. You were real kind."

"You're welcome! Get well soon."

Kevin stopped in the doorway. "You couldn't tell me if *he* lives in the apartment house at the bottom of the street?"

"No, honey. I can't do that. Bye!" and she went inside and shut the door.

Kevin looked in every direction. There was no sign of the Oldsmobile. He walked fast until he reached Eighth Avenue. There, right on the corner, was the Oldsmobile. He noticed that there was a bus stop on the other side of the road, for buses going uptown. He hid in a doorway and waited, hoping the driver had not seen him. A few moments later, the stop lights said 'Walk', and he ran across the road just in time to jump on a bus before it moved off. Suddenly he remembered that the fare box only took coins. As on the subway, 50 cents would take him anywhere in New York, but unless he had exactly 50 cents, the bus driver would tell him to get off. He had only one quarter and a few nickels, but with his eyes on the Oldsmobile, he held out a dollar bill to the driver.

"I don't give change," the driver said.

Kevin looked behind him. The Oldsmobile had made a U-turn and was moving slowly forward, keeping just behind the bus.

"Oh, I didn't know that," Kevin lied.

The driver gave him a quick look. "You're a Canadian, aren't you?"

Before Kevin could answer, a girl got up and offered him a quarter and some dimes and nickels for his dollar bill. Kevin thanked her, and dropped the two quarters in the box, but he did not sit down. The driver shut the door and the bus moved off. The Oldsmobile followed. They went round Columbus Circle, but after a few blocks there was a traffic jam. A yellow cab had stopped in the middle of the Avenue and the driver was examining the engine. Kevin looked through the window and saw the trees of Central Park rising above the traffic. He could only just see the hood of the Oldsmobile and knew that the bald-headed black could not see him.

"Can I get off here?" he begged the driver.

"It's not a stop."

Central Park with the Hudson River and the George Washington Bridge in the background

Grand Army Plaza, where Kevin hid

"Please, I've got to get off!"

The driver looked at the cuts on his face. "What have you done to yourself?"

"I fell over."

"You should go to a doctor."

"*Please,* will you open the door?"

"O.K., but be quick. This traffic jam isn't going on for ever. Here's a transfer. You may need one."

Kevin took the piece of paper. He was glad to have the transfer, because it meant he could get on another bus without having to spend any money. He crossed the road, walking through the jam of cars. As he entered the Park, he looked round. He could not see the Oldsmobile anywhere. With luck, the driver had not seen him get off the bus. He walked straight to the lake and sat down on the grass, choosing a place where there were other people. In summer the lake was crowded, but today there were only two or three rowboats on the dark water. An elegantly dressed girl rode by on horseback. At any other time, he would have enjoyed sitting in Central Park. It was a great sports center and playground for millions of New Yorkers. It was at the ice rink here that he had learned to skate, and he had many times rowed on the lake. Little children screamed as they ran after each other round the great, gray rocks. New York was built on rock, but the only rock to be seen now was in Central Park. Two joggers ran by in open-neck shirts. Two old people were finishing their lunch on the grass beside him. The man got up and threw the plastic cups and plates into a trash can. Most Americans like public places to be clean and do not leave trash on the ground.

A half-hour later, Kevin got up. There was no sign of the black with the bald head. He decided to walk across the Park down the broad, tree-lined Mall. As he neared the Zoo at the far end, he happened to look round. The Mall was full of people. But among them he saw a bald black head. He began to run – past the Zoo and out the Park into the Grand Army Plaza. People were still sitting round the statue in the middle of the Plaza finishing their picnic lunches. He sat down among them and looked across to the Park. The heads of the two young people in front of him were so close together that he could not possibly be seen. This time he had a good view of the black. His face was black, and he was bald, but he had the nose and lips of a white man. He was tall and looked strong, and he was well-dressed and wore a pair of gloves. Kevin was sure he would recognize him if he saw him again.

The man's eyes were searching the sidewalk. For some reason, he did not think of looking at the statue. Cars and cabs were stopping in front of the Plaza Hotel, one of New York's most expensive hotels. Kevin thought of hiding in the hotel. You can walk into most hotels in New York without being stopped by the doorman. He looked back at the Park. The man had gone. But he could be anywhere, and still waiting for him. Kevin was afraid to return to Greenwich Village at once. He did not want the man to discover where he lived. He was thinking not only of himself, but also of Aunt Bella.

He quickly crossed the road into Fifth Avenue and walked uptown, past the tall apartment houses where many of the rich New Yorkers lived. He looked behind him every few minutes. Why had the man tried to kill him? Kevin's eyes searched everywhere, but he could not see any bald-headed blacks. At last he turned round and walked back again. The black had disappeared.

From Fifty-ninth Street downwards, Fifth Avenue has some of the smartest and most expensive stores in Manhattan. A young woman came out of a store wearing smart new clothes and with diamond rings on her fingers. Kevin wandered about midtown Manhattan, past modern skyscrapers which he found very beautiful. They were all so different from each other. Every few minutes he hid in a doorway as close to the entrance as possible. Once he hid for five minutes in a sub-

Fifth Avenue

way station, but the black did not appear. Tired and anxious, he went down into one of the underground shopping malls. It was good to escape from the traffic, and he walked through the mall until he reached a café on a terrace where there were small trees and running water. The sun streamed through a glass roof high above him. He sat down on a chair and ordered a coke, which he drank slowly. He looked around him, but could not see the black. He began to feel better. His neighbor was a middle-aged man with rather long hair and an old jacket. Opposite him sat an elegant young woman with her smart little

New York – Manhattan Island

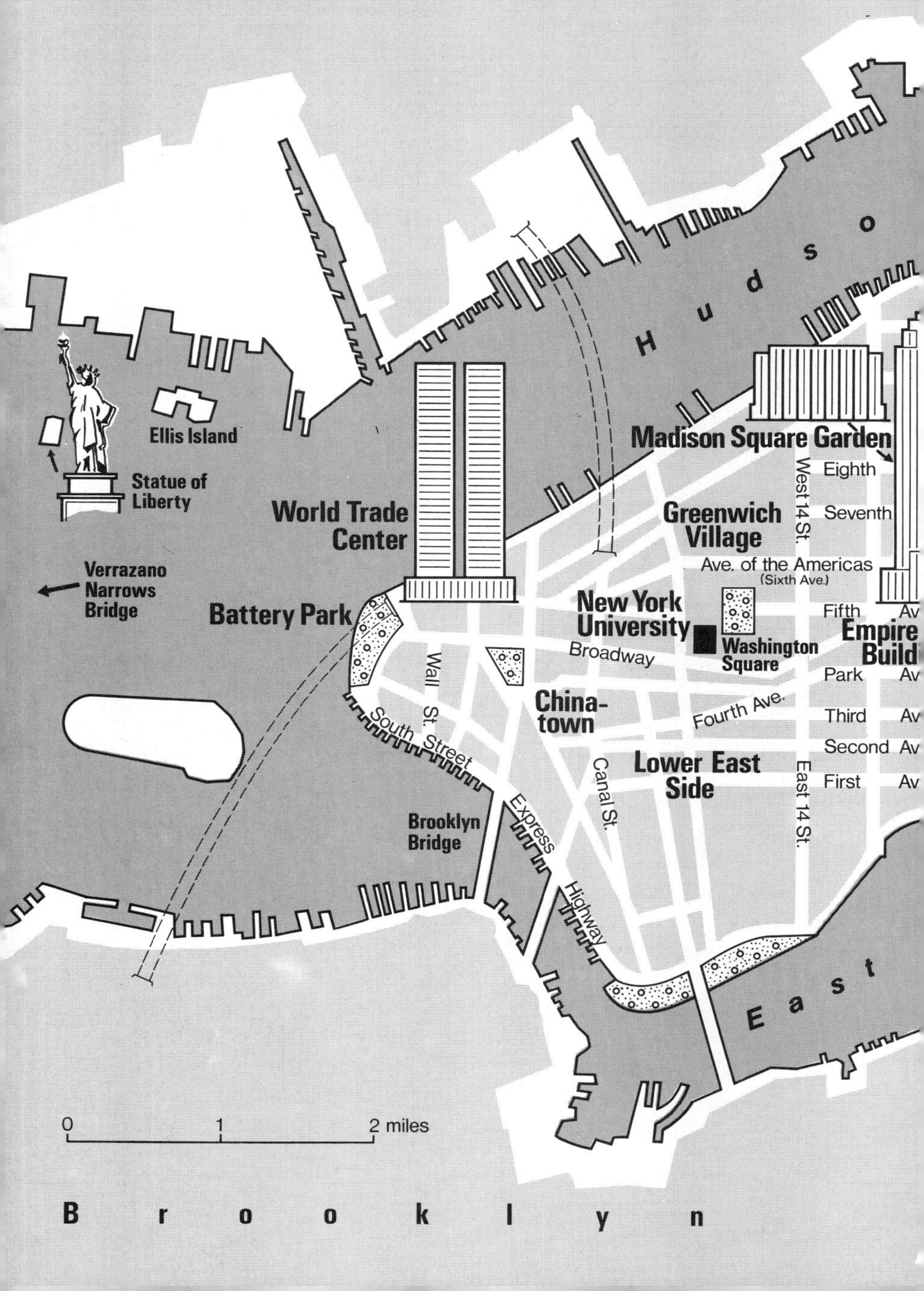

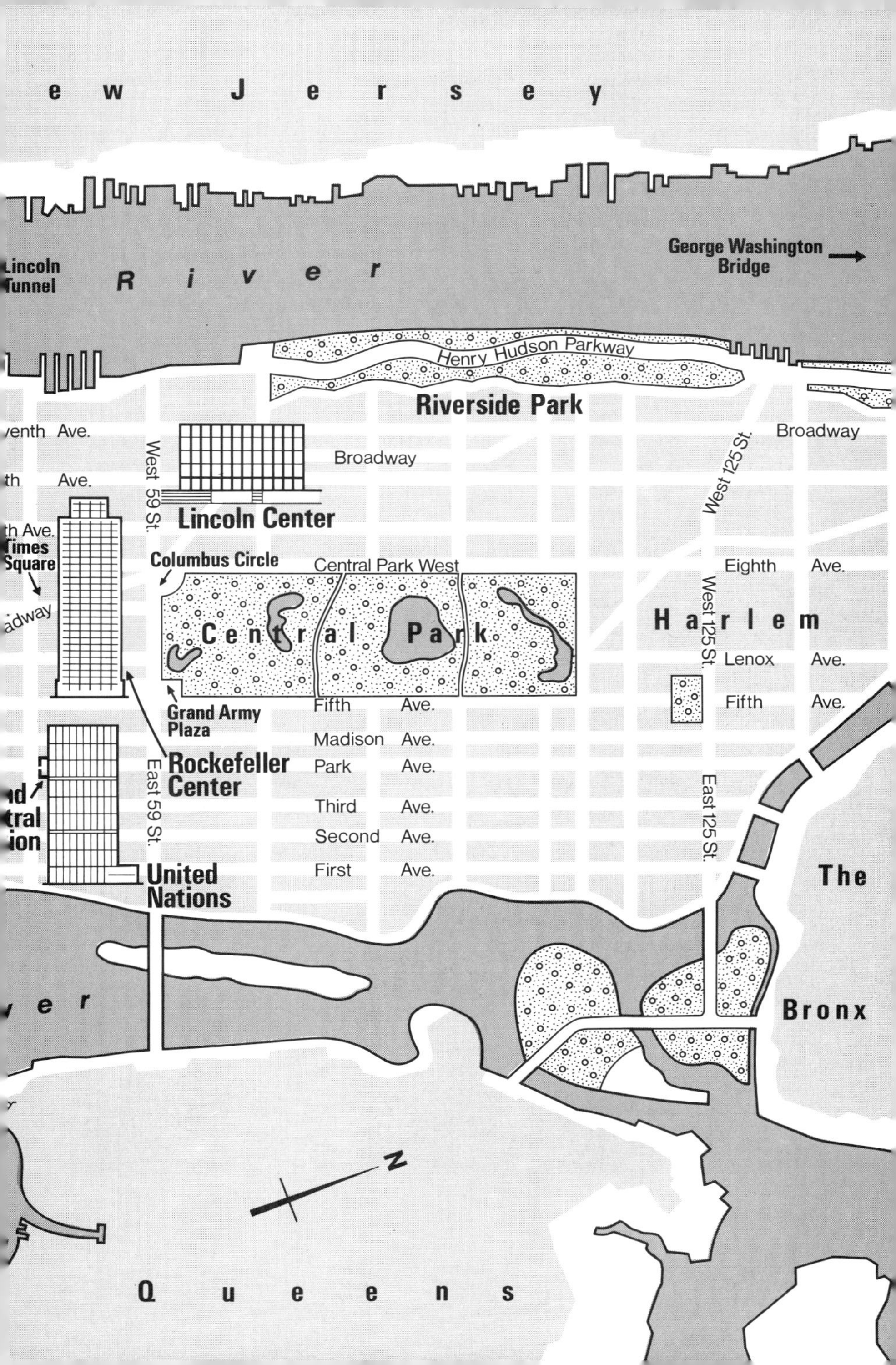

ew Jersey
River
Lincoln
Tunnel
George Washington
Bridge
Henry Hudson Parkway
Riverside Park
venth Ave.
th Ave.
th Ave.
Broadway
West 59 St.
Lincoln Center
West 125 St.
Broadway
Times
Square
adway
Columbus Circle
Central Park West
Central Park
Eighth Ave.
West 125 St.
Harlem
Lenox Ave.
Fifth Ave.
Grand Army
Plaza
Fifth Ave.
Madison Ave.
Park Ave.
Third Ave.
Second Ave.
First Ave.
Rockefeller
Center
East 59 St.
East 125 St.
nd
tral
ion
United
Nations
The
Bronx
ver
N
Queens

girl. The café itself was smart, but the prices were not high and anybody could sit there as long as they liked.

At last Kevin decided to go home. When he reached the subway station, he hid once more near the entrance. He stayed in hiding for ten minutes, but the black still did not appear. When he got home, Aunt Bella was there and he told her what had happened.

"You'll have to go to the police, darling. This isn't the kind of job for boys. Look at those cuts on your face!"

"I haven't enough evidence to give the police, Auntie. The black woman who saw him try to kill me said she wouldn't give evidence against him. She hates him, I'm sure, but she's afraid. The security guard doesn't know anything, I think. The police just wouldn't believe someone like me."

"Well, I don't think you ought to go near that apartment house again."

"I won't, Auntie – at least not for the next few days. I'm starting work on Monday."

An underground shopping mall

5. The Guide

On Monday Kevin arrived early at the office. Mr. Swift was there to welcome him and decided to tell him about some of the people and the problems he might meet. Mr. Swift then acted the part of a dumb tourist who asked stupid questions, and after that the part of a tourist who thought he knew more than the guide. Mr. Swift liked the way Kevin answered all the questions. Kevin was quick and he had a nice sense of humor. He also knew a lot about New York.

"Your aunt was right. She always is!" he said. "And you seem to know New York as well as a New Yorker. Still, for the first week I'm putting you with Mrs. Richter – or Debbie, as we call her. You'll like her, and she'll help you a lot."

For the first few days, Kevin hardly had time to think about Cathy, though once or twice his heart almost stopped when he thought he saw the bald-headed black. He enjoyed the job. He soon became friends with pretty, young Debbie Richter, who invited him to supper to meet her husband, Earle. One day Debbie and Kevin had to take a party of Texans up the Empire State Building. At Debbie's suggestion, Kevin did the talking. "It will give you practice," she said.

"O.K.," he said.

He felt a little nervous at first, but not for long.

"You folks think it's the tallest building in New York, right? . . . No? Well done, sir! The tallest building *is* the World Trade Center. See those two towers over there, near the Harbor? That's it. But this old girl held the record for over thirty years – the tallest building in the world. . . . Yes, sir, there *are* two skyscrapers in Chicago taller than the World Trade Center. They'll be reaching the moon before long!"

The express elevators in the Empire State Building are very fast. They travel eighty floors in less than one minute.

"Oh, dear!" one old lady cried.

"Don't worry, ma'am!" Kevin said. "This elevator has never in all its life killed a Texan!"

When it was all over, Debbie laughed. "You act the clown very well," she said. "They liked you!"

That evening he decided to risk it and go back to the apartment house on Eleventh Avenue. He told Aunt Bella, who tried to persuade him not to go. This time he walked up and down the far side of the

The Empire State Building

Avenue for an hour. He hoped that he might see Cathy, or possibly the bald-headed black. He had on different clothes and was wearing a cap, and as it was getting dark, he did not think the man would recognize him. He had just decided to leave, when a young black boy dressed in smart clothes got out of a large chauffeur-driven limousine and walked up and down the sidewalk not far from the apartment house. The boy could hardly be more than fourteen. A moment later, the bald-headed black came through the lobby doors. He was about to stop a cab, when he saw the limousine on the other side of the road. He ran across the road and began to shout at the boy angrily. At last the boy, after looking anxiously up and down the sidewalk, persuaded the bald-headed black to get into the limousine. Kevin moved back into a doorway as the car drove off.

He walked home slowly, thinking of all the things he had seen and heard. He was beginning to fit together what he knew and to try and make some sense of it all: He knew Cathy was in some kind of trouble and that she was afraid of her stepmother. Why? And why didn't Cathy's stepmother want Cathy to see him? Perhaps she was afraid Cathy would tell him something – but what? Why, of course, something about her stepmother! Well, certainly Cathy's stepmother didn't have very pleasant friends – that bald black, for example, who had tried to kill him. So this 'something' about Cathy's stepmother must be quite serious. Kevin thought again about the young black boy in the big limousine. The way he acted was suspicious, too. In fact anyone who knew that creepy bald guy must be suspicious. But what was going on?

* * * * * *

Next day he told Aunt Bella over a quick cup of coffee what he had seen and what he had thought about the night before.

Aunt Bella looked worried. "Listen, honey," she said, "this sounds real bad. I think your Mrs. O'Brien has something to do with a drugs gang. It all fits, and this last piece of information makes me doubly sure. That kid, with the smart clothes and the big car, sounds like one of the teenage pushers who are so big in New York just now."

"But a teenager, Auntie!"

"Don't be surprised, Kev. Because they're teenagers, they think they'll have an easier time in the courts, so they're prepared to risk anything. They can make a fortune. Why, I heard of one Puerto Rican girl who's only eighteen and she lives in a big apartment, wears the smartest clothes, has a chauffeur-driven car, everything." Aunt Bella's voice was serious. "Please be very careful, honey."

That day Kevin and Debbie took a large party on a visit to the World Trade Center, speeding to the top in the express elevators. Kevin could find little to say this time as he was thinking about what Aunt Bella had told him, so Debbie did the talking. Their instructions were to go afterwards to the Statue of Liberty. The boat left every hour from Battery Park, a small public garden right at the end of Manhattan. On the way to Battery Park they walked down the narrow canyon of Wall Street, the world-famous business center of New York. About twenty of the younger members of the party said they were sure one of the great banks was a palace, and they marched in to have a look.

"I know they're only having fun, but get 'em out, Kev!" Debbie said.

"Come on, all of you!" Kevin said sharply. "You're not welcome here. Please get out at once!"

A woman in a gray coat was standing at one of the counters. She was holding a thick wad of dollar bills – Kevin guessed they were hundred dollar bills. His eyes met hers. It was Mrs. O'Brien. There was no doubt that Mrs. O'Brien was startled by this unexpected meeting. Kevin stared at the wad of bills and then left.

When they reached Battery Park, Kevin and Debbie sat down, glad of the twenty minutes they would have to wait for the boat. Some of the

Verrazano Narrows Bridge

party went down to the water's edge and pointed out the sights. Others lined up at the Park's comfort station. A large cruise ship was just passing under the great suspension bridge of the Verrazano Narrows, on its way out to the Atlantic. Debbie was staring at Ellis Island, which lay between Manhattan and New Jersey. They looked at each other.

"You're very dreamy today, Kev. What are you thinking of?" Debbie asked.

"You tell me what you're thinking about first," Kevin said.

"I was remembering what Earle's grandmother told me about Ellis Island – how awful it was. She was a German from Cologne."

During the late nineteenth and early twentieth centuries, altogether eight million immigrants were held on Ellis Island, waiting their turn with the doctors. Few of these immigrants could speak English. The overworked doctors, who were not always kind, had to examine each one of them, because no one who was ill was allowed into the U.S.A.

"Earle's grandmother had an infectious disease. They let her through in the end, but her brother, who had nothing the matter with him, was sent back to Germany because he coughed once or twice."

"Well, it's an historic monument now," Kevin said.

There must have been pretty Irish immigrants who looked like Cathy, Kevin thought, and some of them must have had a hard time. The Irish were not at all liked at first in New York. Most of them were uneducated and very poor, and all of them had a bitter hatred of the English.

At that moment the boat for the Statue of Liberty came in, and they got up.

"I'm a bad sailor," an old lady said. "Do you think I'll be sick?"

"Look at the water, ma'am," Kevin said without a smile. "It's as calm as a lake."

They all hurried to get places on the boat.

"Kevin, what's the matter with you today? What's happened to your sense of humor?"

"I don't have a sense of humor today," he said. "I'm very worried, Debbie. I'll tell you about it when we're free."

When they landed, an old man came up to them. "Do you think I could walk to the top?" he asked.

"No, I wouldn't if I were you," Debbie said. "There are 167 steps. I'd take the elevator. You'll have quite a few steps to climb when you leave the elevator."

A small boy ran up to Kevin. "Can I climb up the torch?" he asked.

"Sure," Kevin replied, "but first see if you can reach the top of the lady's crown before us. Come on, Debbie!"

Kevin led the way. At the top, people crowded round him to ask questions.

"Who built the statue?"

"It was a gift from the French."

"The French? Why the French?"

"As a mark of friendship between the two countries."

"I didn't know there was any friendship!"

"You look surprised! The French helped the Americans against the British in the Revolutionary War, you know."

"Was it built, then, immediately after the Revolutionary War?"

"No, not until 1886."

They returned to Battery Park, where a bus was waiting for them. When the bus had delivered them all to their hotels, Debbie said to Kevin, "It's 6.30. Let's go and have something to eat at a fast food restaurant. Then you can tell me what's worrying you."

The place was clean and cheap. Debbie and Kevin stood at the counter.

"Beefburgers?" Kevin asked.

"O.K.," Debbie replied.

"Beefburgers and French fries for two," Kevin said. "And two coffees."

"To go?" the girl asked.

"No, to eat here."

The food was passed over the counter in cardboard boxes. The knives and forks were plastic, and so were the coffee cups. There were trash cans in the restaurant into which the customers threw everything left at the end of the meal, including all the plastic material.

They sat down at a table against the wall. While they were eating their beefburgers, Kevin told Debbie everything that had happened since his meeting with Cathy at Niagara Falls. She listened without saying a word. Then suddenly she said in a low voice, "Don't look, but there's a

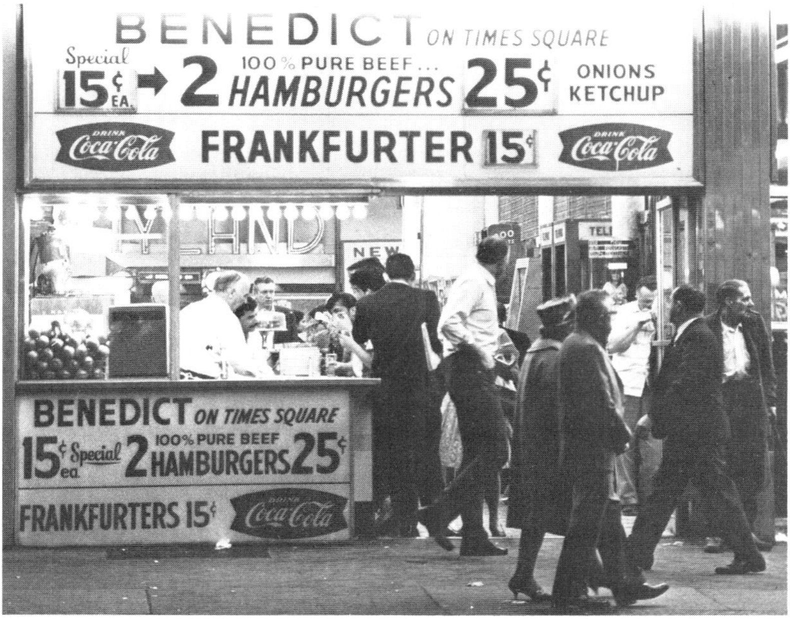

Fast food restaurant

bald-headed black sitting at a table on the other side of the room. He's with a strange-looking kid who can't be more than fourteen or fifteen. But he's wearing a smart business suit, and he's smoking a big cigar!"

Kevin kept his voice low. "That's Baldie all right! The kid must be the pusher he rode off with in the limousine last night."

"But a kid of that age!"

"I know. I told my Aunt Bella about the kid and the chauffeur-driven car. She said that teenage pushers take risks because they think they won't be sent to prison. She said they can make fortunes."

Debbie suddenly picked up all the trash from the table and went over to the trash can which stood a few feet from the black's table. She pushed the pieces in one by one, very slowly, plates, cups, knives, forks, spoons. Then she came and sat down again. Kevin had kept his face turned to the wall.

"Baldie's name is Johnnie," she said in a low voice. "Johnnie said to the kid, 'Meet you at the "house" then, at 8 o'clock'."

"He didn't say where?"

"No," Debbie replied. "The kid's just gone out the door, and Johnnie's getting ready to leave."

Kevin leaned across the table. "Debbie," he said, "Johnnie once followed me. Now I'm going to follow him."

"Kev! That's dangerous and stupid. Why don't you go to the Precinct and ask to talk to the Lieutenant? People are often very unfair about the cops. They do a difficult job, and they do it well."

"I'll go when I'm ready, Debbie. I just don't have enough evidence yet. Anyway, there's one thing that worries me terribly. Does the stepmother know that Cathy knows? If she does, then Cathy could be in awful danger. She and her stepmother hate each other – I'm sure they do. It doesn't seem as if Cathy's been to the police. I'd like to know why. It could be something she's afraid of, Debbie. Could you call my aunt if I'm not . . . "

"Kev, he's getting up now!" She put her hand on his. "Be sensible, if that's possible. He's just thrown his trash into the trash can, and now he's going out the door."

"Thanks a lot, Debbie," Kevin said, getting up. "Be seeing you!"

"I'll call your aunt, Kev. Bye! And good luck!"

Madison Square Garden

6. A Trip to Harlem

Johnnie was walking uptown along the sidewalk. Finally he turned up West 34th Street and went into Madison Square Garden, where a big boxing match between two heavyweight blacks was going to take place the following evening. Kevin had often been to this big sports arena to watch basketball and hockey matches. Johnnie came out again. He looked angry, and Kevin guessed that there were no tickets left. Johnnie walked up Seventh Avenue to Broadway and Times Square. In Times Square he examined the advertisements outside the movie theaters and then finally entered the subway. Kevin followed him and got into the next car without being seen. But after a few stations they were already in Harlem, and he had the unpleasant feeling that he was the only white in the car. In the corner on the other side of the car there were two big black youths who kept looking at him and talking to one another in a low voice.

Kevin had seen the Harlem ghetto once from a train that was on its way to Grand Central Station. It had shocked him. The place looked as if it had been heavily bombed. Whole blocks of buildings had been burned, but their blackened walls still stood, and from the lights inside, Kevin knew that some families still lived there.

At last, at 125/Lenox Avenue, Johnnie got out. The two young blacks got out too, and ran up the steps in front of Kevin. Johnnie walked away from the station. Kevin hesitated a second before following him. He was now in the middle of Harlem, and it was getting dark. This was the black ghetto of New York, where whites were warned not to go. Many of the blacks had no job, and life in this awful slum often drove them to despair. In their despair, some of the young ones took drugs. When they needed money to buy drugs, they often mugged people. Kevin had learned this from Aunt Bella, who, like Debbie, had warned him to keep out of Harlem. "They're dangerous because they're in despair," Aunt Bella had said, "and there is nobody they can go to for help. It's not safe for whites to go there. It's not their fault – but I don't want you hurt, darling."

Kevin was glad he did not have far to go. Johnnie entered a house, smaller than most, one block from the station. There was a street lamp in front of the door, so that Kevin could see quite clearly the comings and goings. A large yellow Mercedes stopped under the street lamp. A girl in a leather coat got out. She turned her head, and Kevin saw that she could not be more than sixteen. Altogether ten people walked through the door, and all of them were certainly under twenty-one. So this must be the meeting the black kid had told Johnnie about in the fast food restaurant.

Kevin made a note of the number of the house and turned back to the subway station. Two young blacks stood in the entrance and stopped him from going in. They were the youths he had seen in the subway car.

"O.K., pretty boy. Let's have it – all you have!"

Kevin stared from one to the other.

"Come on!" one of them said.

"O.K." Kevin said, "but my bill-fold is empty."

He put his hand in his pocket, pulled out a Swift's Tours brochure and threw it on the ground. At the same time he pushed them back and rushed between them. He had his token ready, but just as he reached the turnstiles, he saw a black policeman.

"I'm being mugged!" he cried. "They're close behind me!"

The two youths came round the corner, the policeman put out his arms and caught them both. By this time, Kevin was on his way down to the trains.

When he reached home soon after 9.30, Aunt Bella was out. He made himself a cup of hot chocolate and sat down on the couch. Did Cathy's stepmother really have something to do with a heroin gang? If so, he must find Cathy quickly. He took her key from his pocket. He felt quite sure now that it was the key to her apartment. He'd find a way to get in. He must, he had to. By the time Aunt Bella came in, he had gone to bed.

The following day Kevin was free. Aunt Bella had just gone out, when the telephone rang. He picked up the receiver. A girl's voice said, "Hello! Who's that?"

"Kevin Patterson speaking."

"It's Cathy, Kevin. Do you remember? We met at the coffee shop in Niagara Falls."

"Do I remember you, Cathy! You know I do! I've been having quite an interesting time trying to find you again!"

She spoke fast, telling him what had happened to her since. She had discovered that her stepmother was a kind of go-between in the heroin business – between the big boss who smuggled the stuff from Europe, and the black who sold it to pushers in Harlem.

"Is he bald, and has he white blood in him?"

"Yes! How on earth did you know that?"

She sounded frightened. He told her in a few words what had happened to him.

"Are you in any danger, Cathy?"

"No – not yet – but I'm afraid to call the police, because my stepmother has threatened to kill my brother. She has connections in Charleston."

"How did you find out that she was in the heroin racket?"

"It was between school and Niagara. She had to stop several times at a gas station to go to the restroom. She wasn't feeling at all well, and once she forgot to take her bag with her. It was open, so I looked inside, and I saw a letter. Of course I read it. I had always been suspicious that she was a crook, and in the letter I learned we were going to meet the big boss himself in Montreal, the man she gets the heroin from."

"You have his name and address?"

"Yes."

"Wonderful! Where are you calling from, Cathy?"

"From the apartment. She locks me in, and I can't open the door from the inside. And she told me that if I used the phone, she'd know every word I said, because the room is bugged. I searched and searched, and today I found the bug. It's very, very small. I've taken it down and hidden it somewhere where it can't hear anything! It's O.K., I'm sure, but I'll have to put it back."

"But how did you know my phone number?"

"I remembered that you'd said something about Swift's Tours. I called them. You weren't there, so they gave me your home number."

"Cathy, tell me, is Johnnie, the bald-headed black, your stepmother's partner?"

"Yes. He lives on the floor below us."

"I have your key, Cathy. You left your bag in the coffee shop, remember?"

"Yes. I guessed you must have it. It's a special key to the apartment. She gave it me about two years ago, when we were 'friends'. Now, Kev, I've something very important to say. I've written it down, so I won't forget it. If you don't want to do what I ask, you must say so honestly."

"I'll do it, Cathy!"

"No, wait, Kev. Do you have a pencil and paper?"

"Yes."

"I'll speak very slowly so that you can write it all down. All of what I'm going to say is true. I've done lots of detective work."

"O.K., Cathy. I'm listening."

"My stepmother is going to meet the plane from Montreal at Kennedy Airport tomorrow, where she'll collect a packet of heroin from the big boss. She'll leave here at about 10 o'clock, and should be back at 11.30. She'll visit Johnnie in his apartment first. Then she'll come up here. Johnnie will go straight to a house in Harlem, where he'll sell the stuff to the pushers. I want you to take all this information to the police, Kev. My only worry is, will they believe you?"

"My Aunt Bella – she's the aunt I'm living with – knows the Lieutenant at the Precinct. She'll arrange things. Don't worry, Cathy. Everything will be all right. I wish I could use your key and come and see you at once, just to tell you not to worry."

"No, for Heaven's sake! Keep right away. Don't forget, Johnnie's downstairs, and he knows you."

"Gosh, Cathy! Aren't you frightened?"

"Sometimes. But, Kev – don't, *please* don't forget to tell the police about my brother. That's terribly important."

"I won't, Cathy."

"Will we meet afterwards, Kev?" Cathy asked a bit anxiously.

"What a silly question!" Kevin said. "Bye, Cathy! It was great to hear your voice. Don't worry!"

He sat down on the couch and thought for a long time. Then he picked up the receiver and called Debbie's number.

"Debbie, do you think Mr. Swift would give us a holiday tomorrow?"

"You've forgotten. We have a holiday anyway. The French party hasn't arrived yet because of a strike at Orly. Remember?"

"Debbie, could you possibly help me tomorrow – meet me with your car in Washington Square at 9 o'clock?"

"Sure, Kev. What's it all about?"

"Cathy and her stepmother. We're going to tell the police."

"How can I help you?"

"Just drive me to a place where I can see what happens."

"Is that sensible, Kev?"

"I don't see why not. I'm not going to do anything. But I guess it could be dangerous. I never thought of that. Forget I asked you, Debbie!"

"No, Kev," she said quickly. "I'll be in Washington Square at 9 o' clock."

"But what about Earle, Debbie? What'll he say if it's going to be dangerous?"

"Don't worry. Earle and I, we each do what we like. It'll be all right, Kev. See you at 9 o'clock."

"O.K. It's a hundred to one we'll just sit and wait. Bye!"

When Aunt Bella came home an hour later, he told her what had happened. She hesitated.

"I know you, Kevin. You tell the truth. But . . . "

"What I've told you is completely true, Auntie."

Aunt Bella thought for a moment. Then she said, "Of course I'll call my friend the Lieutenant and tell him he must see you."

Kevin laughed. "I sure hope he does!"

Aunt Bella called the Precinct and asked for the Lieutenant. "Herb? Is that you? It's Bella speaking . . . No! I'm not calling you about the Puerto Ricans again . . . It may well be something more serious."

A half-hour later, Kevin was sitting at a table in the Precinct talking to the Lieutenant. The room was large, and there were policemen everywhere writing reports, typing, shouting at one another, drinking coffee. It was just like a scene from a TV police drama. Kevin told the

Precinct house

Lieutenant everything he knew. The Lieutenant listened silently while another policeman took notes.

"Will you be able to get into the apartment easily?" Kevin asked anxiously.

"No problem!" the Lieutenant replied. "That'll be the first thing we do after Mrs. O'Brien has left for the airport."

"That's the best bit of news you've given me!" Kevin said, putting his hand into his pocket to see if Cathy's key was still there. He felt guilty that he had not told the Lieutenant about the key.

"We'll call the Charleston police at once," the Lieutenant said, "and put Cathy's brother under police protection." He got up and put his hand on Kevin's shoulder. "That was a very good report you gave. Ever thought of becoming a policeman?"

"Sometimes, yes," Kevin replied.

7. Things go wrong

Kevin woke early. He put on his strongest shoes and a leather jacket and sat down to breakfast with Aunt Bella.

"The Lieutenant asked me if I'd like to be a policeman," he said.

"Herb reads character well," his aunt said. "Maybe he read yours."

Kevin finished his coffee and got up.

"Keep well away, Kev," his aunt said. "Remember, they know who you are."

"I'll try, Auntie," Kevin said, and set off for Washington Square. Debbie was already there, waiting in her car.

They had nearly reached Eleventh Avenue, when they heard the sound of police sirens. It was quite usual to hear sirens in New York, but this time there were not only police cars but also several ambulances. When they reached Eleventh Avenue, Debbie stopped the car on the other side of the road, opposite the apartment house. Further up the Avenue, there were crowds in the street, and the police were stopping all traffic.

"Must be a bad road accident," Debbie said.

They sat and waited. They had a perfect view of the entrance to the apartment house. At five after ten, Mrs. O'Brien left, carrying a large bag. A moment or two later, a man in a dark raincoat came out of a doorway and followed her up the street.

"It's started, Debbie!" Kevin said. "In a minute you'll see a plain clothes policeman enter the lobby. After that, I don't know what's going to happen. The Lieutenant didn't tell me."

They waited. They heard the sound of sirens, but no traffic came up the Avenue. There was a strange quiet. The street leading to Tenth Avenue was empty. It was getting hot, but at Debbie's suggestion, they kept the windows up.

"When the sun is shining on the glass," she said, "they won't be able to see us."

As the minutes passed, Kevin kept looking at his watch. At last he said, "Something's wrong. It's almost 10.45. A few women have come out the lobby doors. That's all. Nobody has gone into the building."

"What are you going to do? Call the Precinct?"

"No. I'm going in there myself – if you'll help me."

"Me? What can I do?"

"Something very important, Debbie. If you could go into the lobby and persuade the security guard to come out and have a look at your car . . . "

"But there's nothing wrong with my car."

"We could loosen the leads to the plugs."

"You think if he came out you'd have enough time to get in and past the turnstiles?"

"Sure!"

"And what happens if you meet Johnnie? He may have a gun."

"I've learned a bit of karate, Debbie! Anyway, I don't think he'd shoot, because of the noise. And I'm sure he'll be staying in his apartment until Mrs. O'Brien returns."

"But how are you going to get out again?"

"Please call the police as soon as you can. Tell them I'm in the apartment with Cathy, and we can't get out until they come. Find out what's happened at the Precinct."

"O.K., Kev. Anything you say, sir!"

Kevin lifted the hood of Debbie's car and loosened the leads. Then he waved to Debbie, crossed the road and stood close to the wall in the empty street. He was only a few feet from the glass doors. A few moments later, Debbie walked into the building. She was there longer than he had expected, but he could hear laughter and soon afterwards she crossed the road with the security guard.

Kevin was inside the lobby in a flash. The gate beside the desk had been left open, and he ran through it to the elevators. He pressed the button for the ninth floor, and in another minute he was fitting the key into the lock of apartment 908. He pushed open the door.

Two arms embraced him. "Kevin! I thought I said, 'Keep away from here'."

"Cathy! Are you all right?"

They sat on the couch and he told her they would have to stay there until the police came. Something had happened – he did not know what – but he was sure the police would be there soon.

"Where's the telephone, Cathy?" he suddenly said.

"It's gone. I don't know if she was suspicious, but today she's taken it right away. Kev – what about my brother?"

"He's under police protection in Charleston. Cathy, that day we met in Niagara Falls, did you see the man your stepmother was visiting in Montreal?"

"No. She stopped on a lonely road and waited until another car arrived. She got into the other car and left me behind with a man to guard me. He didn't say a single word to me until my stepmother got back."

"Then you drove back to New York?"

"No. It was a rented car, you see. We left it at the car rental place in Montreal and went back to New York in the Metroliner."

The time passed quickly. It was 11.45 by the clock on the wall. Suddenly they heard a noise in the passage outside and a key turned in the lock. Before they had time to get up, the door opened and Johnnie stood in front of them. They stared at one another, astonished.

"What the hell are you doin' here?" Johnnie said to Kevin.

"Visiting Cathy," Kevin said as coolly as possible.

"How the hell did you get in? This door don't open from inside without a special key, and she don't have one of those."

"What do you want, Johnnie?" Cathy said.

"Now that's real polite, I must say. A real nice welcome. Why don't you ask me if I'd like to sit down, and would I like a drink? O.K. I'll tell you what I want. Your stepmother's in my apartment downstairs, and she don't feel too good."

"What's wrong with her?"

"Well, I guess she's kind of dead."

"You're a murderer!" Kevin shouted.

"Yes, kid – and she ain't the first – or the last!" He turned and stared at Cathy. "You know where she keeps her dough, Cathy? Show me where it is."

Cathy shook her head and Johnnie moved towards her.

"I don't know, Johnnie!" Cathy cried. "Honestly, I don't know!"

"Well, you'll come and help me find it, now, won't you?"

He took her by the arm. At the same time, Kevin kicked him as hard as possible on the leg. Johnnie roared with pain, dropped Cathy's arm and turned to Kevin. Kevin waited for him, his arms hanging loosely by his sides. Johnnie pulled a knife from his belt, but still Kevin did not move. As Johnnie suddenly rushed at him, Kevin caught his arm, turned him round and hit him with the side of the hand on the back of his neck. Johnnie crashed to the floor, the knife flying from his hand. He lay where he fell, without moving. Kevin went quickly down on his knees and listened to Johnnie's heart.

"He's not dead."

Cathy looked at Kevin with surprise and admiration.

"Gosh!" he said. "I didn't know I'd learnt karate so well!"

"There's someone else in the passage!" Cathy said.

Suddenly the door opened and two men with guns rushed in. One of them pointed at Johnnie on the floor.

"That's the man we want!" he said. He turned to Kevin. "Did you do this?"

"Yes. He was attacking the girl."

"How did you do it? He's a dangerous guy."

"Karate! I learned it at High School, but of course he didn't know that. If he had known, I guess there'd have been a different ending! He told us he'd just killed Mrs. O'Brien, in his apartment."

"Yeah, we know. We're policemen."

"We were expecting you much earlier," Kevin said. "What happened?"

"An accident. Someone driving a stolen car ran into the Lieutenant's car and another police car. People on the sidewalk were hit, too. It was like a battlefield. The Lieutenant was taken to hospital, together with five policemen and five pedestrians. The driver of the stolen car was killed."

8. Cathy comes to stay

"Come in, Cathy," Aunt Bella said. "I expect Kevin has told you that I shall be very pleased to have you come and stay here. You'll want to get a job, I imagine?"

Cathy took off her coat and sat on a chair. Kevin and Aunt Bella sat opposite her on the couch.

"Oh, yes," Cathy said. "I couldn't possibly stay here if I didn't pay for my keep."

"I'm going to stay in New York," Kevin said. "I'm going to apply to become an American citizen."

"Why don't you become a policeman?" Cathy said, laughing.

"I'm thinking of it," he answered seriously.

"Oh, no, Kev! I didn't mean it! It's a dangerous job."

"I'm glad they caught those pushers," Kevin said. "They didn't know what was happening on the West Side, so they were all in the house in Harlem, waiting for Johnnie."

"I hear your stepmother is getting better," Aunt Bella said.

"Yes. Johnnie really thought he had killed her, you know."

"He was too greedy," Kevin said. "He wanted her money as well as all the heroin she had brought back from the airport. It's a good thing they caught the man from Montreal as well."

"You were lucky to escape from Johnnie," Aunt Bella said. "I went to see Herb in hospital, and he told me the man had already killed two heroin addicts, because they had been a trouble to the pushers."

"Did you say *lucky?*" Cathy cried. "You should have seen him! He just got hold of Johnnie's arm, and pulled him round, and then, bang! That was that! He was wonderful!"

Manhattan skyline

Vocabulary

Note on American spelling:
Words ending **-our** in Br.E. are spelt **-or** in Am.E., e.g. color, humor, harbor, neighbor. Words ending in in **-re** in Br.E. are spelt **-er** in Am.E., e.g. center, theater. In Am.E. words formed from a word ending in **-el** usually do not double the **l,** e.g. trav**el,** trave**l**er, trave**l**ing.

Chapter 1

coffee shop (Am.E.) place where you can get coffee and a quick, simple meal.
New York (City) largest city in the USA. With its suburbs it covers parts of New York State, New Jersey and Connecticut. Not the capital of the USA.
Hi! (Am.E.) Hello!
Di [daɪ] short for Diana
Doug [dʌg] short for Douglas
work permit [pɜ:mɪt] Arbeitserlaubnis
to pass sb by an jdm vorbeigehen
stepfather, (stepmother, stepdaughter) Stiefvater, etc.
it was none of his business es ging ihn nichts an
Niagara Falls [naɪ'ægərə] large waterfall on the border between Canada and the USA; name of a Canadian and a US town.
it reminded him that es erinnerte ihn daran, daß . . .
Toronto [tə'rɒntəʊ] Canada's second largest city
heart-shaped herzförmig
fringe [frɪndʒ] Ponyfrisur
forehead Stirn
anxiety [æŋ'zaɪətɪ] Sorge
honest ['ɒnɪst] ehrlich
to be in trouble in Nöten sein
to interfere [ˌɪntə'fɪə] sich einmischen
affairs [ə'feəs] Angelegenheiten
I'd rather not ich würde lieber nicht
vacation [və'keɪʃn] (Am.E.) holiday(s)
out the (window, etc.) (Am.E.) out of the (window etc.)
I guess [ges] (Am.E.) I expect, I imagine
kick Fußtritt
to bring sb up jdn aufziehen
to hesitate ['hezɪteɪt] zögern
Charleston old city in South Carolina
high school (Am.E.) comprehensive school
sure (Am.E.) of course, certainly
middle-aged [ˌmɪdl'eɪdʒd] mittleren Alters
suspiciously [sə'spɪʃəslɪ] mißtrauisch
roar [rɔ:] Donnern
you're darned right! [dɑ:nd] (Am.E.) *etwa:* das kannst du laut sagen!
kid (Am.E.) child
cops (Am.E. slang) policemen, also used in Britain
robber Räuber
check (Am.E.) bill (Rechnung)
maybe perhaps

Chapter 2

to call (Am.E.) to ring up
below unten
Maid of the Mist [meɪd] ship which takes tourists up to the Falls

Immigration Officer [ˌɪmɪˈgreɪʃn] Beamter der Einwanderungsbehörde, der Pässe kontrolliert
truck [trʌk] (Am.E.) lorry
truck-stop (Am.E.) filling station with café, etc., specially for truck drivers
cheerful [ˈtʃɪəfl] fröhlich
New Jersey [ˌnjuːˈdʒɜːzɪ] State west of the Hudson River
55 mph speed limit nobody may drive faster than this on any road in the USA
Greenwich Village [ˈgrenɪdʒ] one of the oldest parts of New York. Narrow streets, antique and art shops, restaurants, small theatres, etc.
George Washington Bridge bridge across the Hudson River, built 1931
be seein' you! (Am.E.) see you soon! (bis bald!)
Hudson River [ˈhʌdsn] about 507 km long; Henry Hudson, English sailor, discovered it in 1609
freeway (Am.E.) motorway on which you do not have to pay
Henry Hudson Parkway fast road along the Hudson River on Manhattan Island
Manhattan [mænˈhætn] an island, central district of New York City; business, shopping and entertainment centre of the city (see map)
Greyhound [ˈgreɪhaʊnd] buses belonging to Greyhound go to every part of the USA, and to Canada and Mexico, and are the cheapest way of travelling
subway [ˈsʌbweɪ] (Am.E.) underground railway; the New York subway carries more passengers each year than any other underground in the world, and runs 24 hours a day
Broadway longest Avenue in Manhattan and only one that is not straight; famous for its theatres and night life
token [ˈtəʊkn] Münze
slot [slɒt] Schlitz
turnstile [ˈtɜːnstaɪl] Drehkreuz
express (train) [ɪkˈspres] Eilzug
track (Am.E.) railway line (Gleis)
rush hour Stoßzeit
car (Am.E.) (railway) carriage
Columbus Circle [kəˈlʌmbəsˌsɜːkl] big traffic circle on s.w. corner of Central Park
Fifth Avenue [ˈævənjuː] has some of the city's smartest and most expensive hotels, shops and flats
over hard (Am.E.) well-cooked egg, fried on both sides
hash browns (Am.E.) fried potatoes, eaten at breakfast
Washington Square famous old square in Greenwich Village
lecture [ˈlektʃə] Vorlesung
New York University largest private university in the USA, near Washington Square
Washington Arch [ɑːtʃ] built 1889, a hundred years after George Washington became first president of the USA in 1789
tree-lined [ˈtriːˌlaɪnd] auf beiden Seiten mit Bäumen gesäumt
apartment (Am.E.) flat (Wohnung)
steps Stufen
second floor Am.E. for Br.E. 'first floor'. The **first floor** in the USA is the 'ground floor' in Britain.
guy [gaɪ] (Am.E.) fellow
purple [pɜːpl] purpur
pants [pænts] (Am.E.) trousers
Puerto Ricans [ˌpwɜːtəʊˈriːkənz] Spanish-speaking people from the Caribbean island of Puerto Rico; some white, some mixed, black and white
to admire [ədˈmaɪə] bewundern
enthusiasm [ɪnˈθjuːzɪæzm] Begeisterung

race Rasse
racist ['reɪsɪst] Rassist
couch [kaʊtʃ] (Am.E.) sofa
upstate New York northern part of N.Y. State
Buffalo ['bʌfələʊ] city in upstate New York near Niagara Falls
honey ['hʌnɪ] (Am.E.) darling
real (kind) (Am.E.) really
neighborhood ['neɪbəhʊd] Nachbarschaft
smart [smɑ:t] elegant, vornehm
West Side all parts of Manhattan between Fifth Avenue and the Hudson River
to murder ['mɜ:də] ermorden

Chapter 3

search [sɜ:tʃ] Suche
Brooklyn Bridge ['brʊklɪn] opened 1883; joins Manhattan to Brooklyn; 1,595 ft. long (486 metres)
folks [fəʊks] (Am.E.) people; used a lot: 'Hi, folks!'
paralyzed ['pærəlaɪzd] gelähmt
Rockefeller Center ['rɒkɪfelə] (see map) business centre and offices with underground restaurants, shops, cafés, etc.; built in 1930s
Harlem ['hɑ:ləm] (see map) where many blacks and Puerto Ricans live; very poor district; many buildings in ruins
ghetto ['getəʊ] Ghetto
Chinatown (see map) where about 10,000 Chinese live; some still speak hardly any English and talk to their children in Chinese
decision [dɪ'sɪʒn] Entschluß
to recognize ['rekəgnaɪz] erkennen
apartment house (Am.E.) building with flats (Br.E. block of flats)
store (Am.E.) shop
story/stories Stockwerk (Br.E. also spelt storey/storeys)
opposite ['ɒpəzɪt] gegenüber
advertisement Am.E. [ˌædvə'taɪzmənt] Br.E. [əd'vɜ:tɪsmənt] Reklame
cruise liner [kru:z] Kreuzfahrtschiff
Lincoln Tunnel [ˌlɪŋkən'tʌnl] built 1937–57; 2,500 metres long, 30 m. below the Hudson River
cab taxi; New York cabs are yellow
Lincoln, Chevelle American cars
lobby ['lɒbɪ] (Am.E.) entrance hall of hotel or apartment house
security guard [sɪ'kjʊərətɪ] Angehöriger des Sicherheitspersonals
lock Schloss
mugging ['mʌgɪŋ] Raubüberfall
identity card [aɪ'dentətɪ] Ausweis
to stare [steə] starren
bald [bɔ:ld] kahl
afterwards nachher
Radio City Music Hall in the Rockefeller Center; seats for more than 6000
Wurlitzer organ ['wɜ:lɪtsə] a cinema organ
the Rockettes [rɒ'kets] since 1926 America's most famous troupe of dancing girls
hot dog (Am.E.) sausage in a bread roll; sold on New York street corners
Times Square area on and around Broadway (see map); some of best, and worst, entertainment places in N.Y. are found here
to tempt [tempt] verlocken
Lincoln Center (for the Performing Arts) group of buildings completed in 1960s round a central plaza (Platz) with trees and water; Metropolitan Opera House, N.Y. State Theater (ballet), Philharmonic Hall (concerts) smaller theatres, Library
gang [gæŋ] Bande
crazy ['kreɪzɪ] (Am.E.) mad (verrückt); also used in Britain

Chapter 4

Precinct ['pri:sɪŋkt] (Am.E.) police station for one area, or **precinct,** of the City
close [kləʊs] dicht
garbage ['gɑ:bɪdʒ] (Am.E.) rubbish;
to lift heben
a half-hour (Am.E.) half an hour
sound [saʊnd] Geräusch
windshield ['wɪndʃi:ld] (Am.E.) windscreen
Oldsmobile ['əʊldzməʊˌbi:l] US car
dust Staub
evidence ['evɪdəns] Beweis
death warrant ['wɒrənt] *hier:* Todesurteil
I never saw nothing (slang) I didn't see anything
king-size bed ['kɪŋsaɪz] (Am.E.) very large double bed; ordinary double beds are 'queen-size'
bathroom (Am.E.) toilet (in a home)
bathtub ['bɑ:θtʌb] (Am.E.) bath
ought to [ɔ:t] should
you're welcome ['welkəm] (Am.E.) – you say this when sb has thanked you for something
uptown (Am.E.) (going) away from the city centre; in Manhattan, going north; the **uptown** area is north of 59th Street, **downtown** is south of 34th Street, **midtown** is in between
to hide [haɪd] sich verstecken
stop lights (Am.E.) traffic lights;
(dollar) bill (Am.E.) (dollar) note
make a U-turn ['ju:tɜ:n] wenden
block [blɒk] (Am.E.) buildings between two streets and two avenues
traffic jam ['træfɪkdʒæm] Verkehrsstau
Central Park completed in the mid-nineteenth century; grass lakes, woods, a zoo, dangerous at night
hood [hʊd] (Am.E.) Motorhaube
to beg (dringend) bitten
quarter, dime, nickel ['kwɔ:tə|daɪm|'nɪkəl] (Am.E.) coins worth: 25 cents, 10 cents and 5 cents
a transfer ['trænsfɜ:] (Am.E.) allows passengers to continue their journey on another city bus without paying again – but is not a return ticket
with luck if he was lucky
elegant ['elɪgənt]
to skate [skeɪt] Schlittschuh laufen
jogger ['dʒɒgə] (Am.E.) jd, der Dauerlauf treibt
trash [træʃ] (Am.E.) rubbish, litter; **trash can:** rubbish basket, bin
Mall [mɔ:l] (Am.E.) broad tree-lined path in the Park; a **mall** is also a shopping area with no traffic
statue ['stætʃu:]
Grand Army Plaza [ˌgrændɑ:mɪ'plɑ:zə] at s.e. corner of the Park (see map)
doorman (Am.E.) Pförtner

Chapter 5

dumb [dʌm] (Am.E.) stupid; has same meaning in Br.E., but more often means 'not able to speak' (stumm)
sense of humor ['hju:mə] Sinn für Humor
Empire State Building ['empaɪə] 1,250 feet high (381 m.) and 102 storeys, (1472 ft. with television mast); world's tallest building for 30 years
Chicago [ʃɪ'kɑ:gəʊ] second largest city in USA; its Sears Tower has 109 storeys, 1454 ft. high (443 m.)
World Trade Center two towers, 1350 feet high (411 m.), 110 storeys; business centre with underground shops, cafés, etc.

Harbor ['hɑ:bə] there are docks on the Hudson River and East River (see map)
ma'am [mæm] (Am.E.) madam (in conversation)
chauffeur-driven ['ʃəʊfə] mit Fahrer
limousine ['lɪmu:zi:n]
to fit (together) zusammensetzen
creepy ['kri:pɪ] (Am.E.) nasty
pusher (Am.E.) someone who sells drugs illegally, often on the streets
teenage ['ti:nˌeɪdʒ]
big (Am.E. slang) successful, important
court [kɔ:t] Gericht
Statue of Liberty ['lɪbətɪ] 300 feet high (91.4 m.) including the pedestal on which the lady stands
Battery Park ['bætərɪ] (see map) takes its name from a small fort built beside the water in 1812; ferry terminal
canyon ['kænjən] Felsschlucht
wad [wɒd] (Banknoten) Bündel
startled ['stɑ:tld] erschreckt
to line up (Am.E.) to queue
comfort station ['kʌmfət] (Am.E.) toilet (public)
Verrazano Narrows [verə'zɑ:nəʊ'nærəʊz] way into New York Harbor; discovered by Italian explorer Giovanni da Verrazano in 1524; suspension bridge across the Narrows is the longest in the world (1980)
Ellis Island ['elɪs] small island close to New Jersey; used for immigrants 1892–1924; open to the public since 1976
immigrant ['ɪmɪgrənt] Einwanderer
infectious disease [ɪn'fekʃəs dɪ'zi:z] ansteckende Krankheit
historic monument [hɪ'stɒrɪk'mɒnjʊmənt] historisches Denkmal
uneducated [ʌn'edju:keɪtɪd] ohne Bildung
bad sailor ['seɪlə] oft seekrank
torch [tɔ:tʃ] Fackel
Revolutionary War [ˌrevə'lu:ʃnərɪ] War of Independence 1775–1783
fast food restaurant (Am.E.) here people order food at a counter and receive it in cardboard or plastic boxes; they can eat it at a table or take it away for a picnic
beefburger ['bi:fˌbɜ:gə] (Am.E.) another word for hamburger
French fries (Am.E.) fried potatoes (Br.E. chips)
to go (Am.E.) to take away (food)
Lieutenant Am.E. [lu:'tenənt] Br.E. [lef'tenənt]

Chapter 6

Madison Square Garden ['mædɪsən] big hall on Seventh Avenue; seats for 20,000; used for boxing, sports matches, conferences, etc.
heavyweight ['hevɪweɪt] Schwergewichtler
basketball ['bɑ:skɪtbɔ:l]
hockey ['hɒkɪ]
Grand Central Station completed 1913, biggest railway station in the world; used every day by hundreds of thousands of people
bill-fold (Am.E.) wallet
heroin ['herəʊɪn]
stuff [stʌf] Stoff, Zeug
how on earth? wie um alles in der Welt . . . ?
to threaten ['θretn] drohen
racket ['rækɪt] (dunkles) Geschäft
gas station (Am.E.) petrol station; 'gas' is short for 'gasoline' (petrol)
restroom (Am.E.) toilet at a gas station
crook [krʊk] Gauner

the room is bugged [bʌgd] im Zimmer befindet sich ein Abhörgerät
Montreal [ˌmɒntrɪˈɔ:l] Quebec Province; Canada's largest city
Kennedy Airport [ˈkenədɪ] New York's main airport
to arrange [əˈreɪndʒ] arrangieren
for Heaven's sake! um Gottes Willen!
Gosh! [gɒʃ] Mensch!
Orly [ˈɔ:lɪ] main airport for Paris, France
truth [tru:θ] Wahrheit
to feel guilty [ˈgɪltɪ] *hier:* Gewissensbisse haben
under police protection [prəˈtekʃn] unter Polizeischutz

Chapter 7

to go wrong schiefgehen
to read sb's character [ˈkærəktə] jds Charakter beurteilen
siren [ˈsaɪrən] Sirene
to loosen [ˈlu:sn] lockern
the leads to the plugs [li:dz/plʌgz] die Leitungen zu den Zündkerzen
karate [kəˈrɑ:tɪ] Karate
to shoot [ʃu:t] schießen
to embrace [ɪmˈbreɪs] umarmen
rented car Mietwagen
car rental Autovermietung
Metroliner (Am. E.) [ˈmetrəʊlaɪnə] Inter-City train
passage [ˈpæsɪdʒ] Gang
astonished [əˈstɒnɪʃt] erstaunt
what the hell! was zum Teufel!
don't open, don't have (black E.) doesn't open, doesn't have
polite [pəˈlaɪt] höflich
dough (Am. E. slang) money
belt Gürtel
to attack [əˈtæk] angreifen
to crash to the floor [kræʃ] schwer zu Boden fallen
battleground [ˈbætlgraʊnd] Schlachtfeld
pedestrian [pəˈdestrɪən] Fussgänger

Chapter 8

to pay for one's keep seinen Unterhalt bezahlen
to apply [əˈplaɪ] beantragen
citizen [ˈsɪtɪzn] Staatsbürger
greedy [ˈgri:dɪ] gierig
addict [ˈædɪkt] Süchtige(r)
to get hold of packen